DISNEP PRINCESS

Help Is on the Way!

A Story About *Dependability*

by **Kristen Behrens**
illustrated by
S.I. International

SCHOLASTIC INC.

New York   Toronto   London   Auckland   Sydney
Mexico City   New Delhi   Hong Kong   Buenos Aires

"We're done, Mushu!" Mulan said triumphantly. "The captain won't find the smallest wrinkle in my uniform during inspection."

"I'm glad you're happy," Mushu groaned. "But dragons are supposed to spit fire, not steam. I'm beginning to wilt."

Published by Scholastic Inc.
90 Old Sherman Turnpike, Danbury, Connecticut 06816.

For information regarding permission, write to:
Disney Licensed Publishing
114 Fifth Avenue, New York, New York 10011.

ISBN 0-7172-6812-8

Designed and produced by Bill SMITH STUDIO.

Printed in the U.S.A.
First printing, January 2004

Mulan patted Mushu's head. "It's for a good cause. The captain has promised a free afternoon for anyone whose tent and uniform pass inspection today. I haven't had any time off in weeks!"

Mulan led the way to her tent. "See? My bed is made, helmet is shining, fighting stick is polished, and I made a new string for my bow."

Mushu held up a mirror so she could see. "And your uniform looks outstanding, thanks to your personal laundry service."

Mulan thought of all the things she could do with her precious afternoon off. Maybe she could ride her horse, Khan, or spend some time on the river with her friends Yao, Ling, and Chien-Po.

*J*ust then Yao entered the tent. "Ping," he began desperately. "Can you help me? I'll never be ready for inspection on time!"

The other soldiers thought Mulan was a boy named Ping. "Sure," she said. "What can I do?"

"Everything!" Yao moaned.

Mulan followed Yao to his tent. She stared in amazement at the mess.

"Okay," she said at last. She rolled up her sleeves. "Let's get to work."

Yao heaved a sigh of relief. "Thanks, Ping. I knew I could count on you."

*T*ogether, Mulan and Yao scrubbed and swept . . .

. . . folded and stored . . .

$\mathcal{A}$nd sharpened and straightened.

"Phew," Mulan said, wiping the sweat from her forehead when they were finally finished.

"You said it, Ping," Yao said. "I couldn't have done it without you."

"You can count on me anytime," Mulan told her friend.

*J*ust as Mulan was about to leave Yao's tent, Ling rushed up to her. His hands were hiding something behind his back.

"Ping, can you help me?" he asked.

"I can try," Mulan said. "What's wrong?"

"*I* had finally finished cleaning my tent," Ling explained. "But when I sat down to rest, I sat on my fighting stick and broke it." Sadly, he held up two broken pieces of wood.

"*I* can't put them back together again,"
Mulan said. "We'll have to make you a new one.
But first, we need to find some wood from
a tree."

Ling heaved a sigh of relief. "I knew I could
count on you, Ping."

"This one's too small," said Mulan.
"This one's too tall," Ling commented.
Suddenly Mulan had an idea. "Follow me!"

"*L*et's look for an old tent," Mulan said. "We can make a fighting stick out of a tent pole."

"Great idea, Ping!" Ling exclaimed.

"Here's one," Mulan said, scooping up an old pole. "Just polish this up."

$\mathcal{M}$ulan was once again on her way back to her tent when she heard Chien-Po yelling her name.

"Ping! Thank goodness I found you," he said breathlessly.

"My uniform shrank when I washed it,"
Chien-Po explained sadly. "Now it doesn't fit."

"Oh no," Mulan said kindly. "Let's see what
we can do."

Chien-Po smiled with relief. "What would I do
without you, Ping?"

"There's no time to make you a new uniform," Mulan said. "The only thing we can do is stretch it." So Mulan and Chien-Po pulled . . .

. . . and tugged . . .

. . . and yanked.

$\mathcal{U}$ntil finally, the uniform *just* stretched across Chien-Po's big belly.

"Oh, Ping, thank you!" Chien-Po cried.

Mulan smiled as she rubbed her sore arms. "I'm glad I could help."

*J*ust then the gong sounded. Inspections were beginning! Mulan raced back to her tent just as Captain Li Shang and the Emperor's special assistant, Chi Fu, began their rounds.

Mulan stood at attention. Her heart was beating so hard that she was sure the captain would hear it. Would she pass?

The captain nodded briefly at her and left. She sighed with relief. She had passed!

"Careful, girl," Mushu gasped. "Now you're giving *me* wrinkles."

Mulan laughed. "Sorry, Mushu! I'm just excited. Thanks for helping. Now if only the others pass, too, we can all have fun together."

"Before anybody has any fun, I could use a little grub. How about getting me . . . I mean us . . . some food?" asked Mushu.

"Always thinking," Mulan said, smiling. "Thinking with your stomach, that is. I'll go and get something for you."

On her way to the mess tent, Mulan was joined by Chien-Po, Ling, and Yao.

"Ping," Chien-Po said to Mulan. "Thank you for your help. We all passed inspection!"

"Wonderful!" Mulan said. "What are you all going to do with your free time?"

"*I*'m going to meditate," Chien-Po replied.

"I'm going to catch the biggest fish that ever swam in the river," said Yao.

"I'm going to think about the girls back home," said Ling dreamily.

"What about you, Ping?" Chien-Po asked.

"I haven't had free time in so long," said Mulan. "I'm not sure what to choose."

"There's no choice to make," said Chi Fu. "You're on kitchen duty, Ping."

"But my turn isn't until tomorrow," Mulan protested.

"Wong is ill. Your name moved up the list," said Chi Fu with a mean smile.

"That isn't fair," Ling said.

"You deserve some fun!" Yao exclaimed.

Ping
Yao
Ling
hien-Po

Mulan's heart sank. She had been looking forward to her free time *so* much.

What would a princess do?

Mulan knew what she had to do. "It made me feel good that you could depend on me today," she said to her friends. "I can't let the whole camp down by running away from my own duty."

She turned and walked into the mess tent.

Mulan sank her arms into the tub of soapy water and began to wash. She tried not to think of her friends and the fun they were going to have.

*S*uddenly a pair of hands joined hers in the tub, then another, and another.

$\mathcal{M}$ulan looked up at her friends and grinned.

"We depended on you today," Yao said.

"And you can depend on us," said Chien-Po.

"We'll be finished in no time," Ling said. "Then
we can *all* go and have some fun."

*H*ours later, Mulan was stretched out on the
soft grass under a tree. With the help of her
friends, she had washed a huge pile of dishes and
chopped a mountain of vegetables so quickly
that all of them still had time to relax.

"*I*'m lucky to have friends I can depend on," Mulan said quietly to Mushu.

"They're lucky they can depend on you," Mushu said. "Thanks for the food, by the way. Even though you took long enough to deliver it, *I* knew I could count on you, too!"

The End